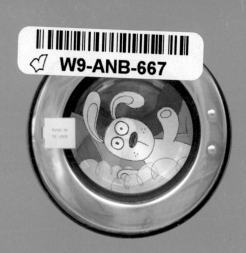

Knuffle Bunny: A Cautionary Musical photographs copyright © 2010 by Carol Pratt

The images in this book are a melding of hand-drawn ink sketches and digital photography on a computer (where the sketches were colored and shaded, the photographs given their sepia tone, and sundry air conditioners, garbage cans, and industrial debris expunged).

First edition with audio CD, 2011.

10 9 8 7 6 5 4 3 2 1

F850-6835-5-10319

Printed in Singapore

Reinforced binding

ISBN 978-1-4231-4449-6

Library of Congress Cataloging-in-Publication Data on file.
Visit www.hyperionbooksforchildren.com and www.pigeonpresents.com

SPECIAL EDITION

KNUFFLE BUNNY

A CAUTIONARY TALE BY Mo Willems

The complete story, plus a CD featuring a storybook read-along and the original cast recording of the Kennedy Center's *Knuffle Bunny: A Cautionary Musical*

HYPERION BOOKS FOR CHILDREN / NEW YORK

An Imprint of Disney Book Group

Not so long ago, before she could even speak words, Trixie went on an errand with her daddy....

Trixie and her daddy went down the block,

past the school,

and into the Laundromat.

Trixie helped her daddy put the laundry into the machine.

She even got to
put the money
into the machine.

Then they left.

But a block
or so later . . .

Trixie **realized**

something.

Trixie turned to her daddy and said,

Blaggle plabble!

Wumby flappy?!

Snurp.

"Now, please don't get fussy,"
said her daddy.

Well, she had no choice.....

Trixie bawled.

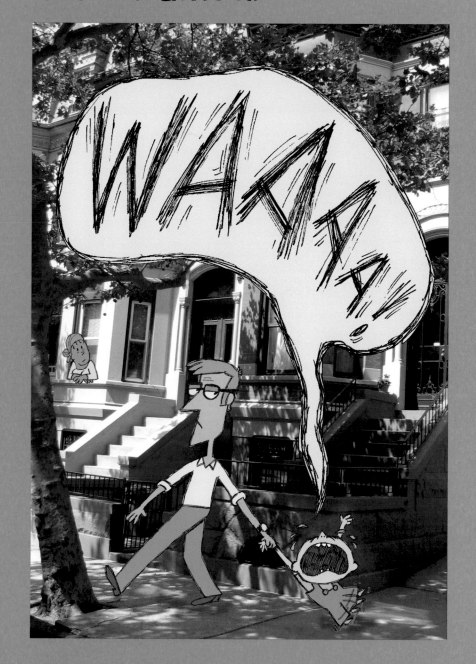

She went boneless.

She did everything she could to show how unhappy she was.

By the time they got home, her daddy was unhappy, too.

As soon as Trixie's mommy opened the door, she asked,

The whole family ran down the block.

And they ran through the park.

They zoomed past the school,

and into the Laundromat.

Trixie's daddy looked for Knuffle Bunny.

And looked . . .

and looked . . .

and looked . . .

But Knuffle Bunny was
nowhere to be found....

So Trixie's daddy
decided to look harder.

Until . . .

And those were the first words Trixie ever said.

This book is dedicated to
the real Trixie and her mommy.
Special thanks to
Anne and Alessandra;
Noah, Megan, and Edward;
the 358 6th Avenue Laundromat;
and my neighbors in Park Slope, Brooklyn.

-Mo

On May 8, 2010,

KNUFFLE BUNNY: A CAUTIONARY MUSICAL

was commissioned by and had its world premiere at the
John F. Kennedy Center for the Performing Arts in Washington, D.C.

Stephanie D'Abruzzo as Trixie

Michael John Casey as Dad

Stephanie D'Abruzzo as Trixie

Script and Lyrics by
Mo Willems

Based on his book
Knuffle Bunny: A Cautionary Tale

Music by **Michael Silversher**
Musical Arrangement by
Deborah Wicks La Puma
Directed by **Rosemary Newcott**

Starring:

Stephanie D'Abruzzo as **Trixie**
Michael John Casey as **Dad**
Erika Rose as **Mom**
and **Matthew McGloin** and **Gia Mora**
as **Puppeteers**

Knuffle Bunny: A Cautionary Musical is a professional
production employing members of Actors' Equity Association.

CD Production Credits

Original Cast CD produced by **Michael Silversher** and **Deborah Wicks La Puma**
Mixing Engineers, **Heidi Gerber** and **Jim Robeson**
Mastering, **Mike Monseur**
Orchestra Recorded at **Crunchynotes Studio**, Rancho Palos Verdes, CA in April 2010
Vocals Recorded at **Bias Studios**, Springfield, VA in August 2010
Mixing done at **All Access Audio**, Silver Spring, MD, and **Bias Studios**
Mastering done at **Bias Studios**

Musical photos by Carol Pratt. Author photo by Cher Willems. Recording studio photo by Jen Howard.

Mo Willems, a number one *New York Times* best-selling author
and illustrator, has been awarded a Caldecott Honor on three occasions.
His celebrated Elephant & Piggie series received two consecutive Theodor
Seuss Geisel Medals. And his picture book debut, *Don't Let the Pigeon
Drive the Bus!*, was one of the first inductees into the Indies Choice
Picture Book Hall of Fame. Other favorites include *Leonardo, the Terrible
Monster* and *Naked Mole Rat Gets Dressed.* Mo began his career on
Sesame Street, where he garnered six Emmy Awards.
   Knuffle Bunny: A Cautionary Musical is Mo's first play. He lives with his family in
Massachusetts and seldom does the laundry.

FROM PAGE TO STAGE

The musical *Knuffle Bunny* began as a book – this book! Mo
Willems, the man who wrote it and drew its pictures, believed
the story could also be told with actors performing and singing
on stage. So, when the Kennedy Center contacted him about
writing a play, he thought of this book and wrote the dialogue
(the words spoken by the characters) and added new parts to the
story, like what Daddy and Trixie see and do on their way to the
Laundromat. He also wrote the lyrics (the words to the songs).
   Other people also helped get the story ready for the stage. A
composer wrote music to go with the songs, and a director chose
the actors. A set designer created the scenery. And puppeteers,
people who work with puppets, crafted several puppets of animals
and other objects. Finally, with lots of practice, everyone was ready
for the show!

The Storybook Read-Along features the voices of Mo, Cher, and Trixie Willems,
with music composed by Scotty Huff and Robert Reynolds.
Production copyright © 2006 by Weston Woods Studios, Inc. All Rights Reserved.

The Education Department of the Kennedy Center has provided quality arts
experiences for students, teachers, families, and the general public throughout the United
States for more than thirty-five years. The mission of the Education Department is to
foster understanding of and participation in the performing arts through exemplary
programs and performances for diverse populations of all ages that represent the
unique cultural life and heritage of the United States. For more information, visit the
Center's Web site at www.kennedy-center.org/education.

Knuffle Bunny at the studio!

TRACKS

1. Overture
2. Tricky with Trixie
3. Walkin' Dad with His Girl
4. Washy Washy
5. Aggle Flaggle Klabble
6. Long Walk
7. Really, Really Love You
8. Run Back
9. Don't Worry
10. Victorious!
11. Knuffle Bunny!
12. Final Scene

BONUS: Storybook Read-Along

Explore the open road
Learn to drive a bus!
No experience necessary

555-4372 555-4372 555-4372 555-4372 555-4372 555-4372 555-4372